SWAMP MONSTER IN THIRD GRADE

Want more books by Debbie Dadey?

Coming soon . . .

The Slime Wars

And don't forget to check out . . .

BY DEBBIE DADEY AND MARCIA THORNTON JONES

SWAMP MONSTER IN THIRD GRADE

BY DEBBIE DADEY
ILLUSTRATIONS BY MARGEAUX LUCAS

A
LITTLE APPLE
PAPERBACK

SCHOLASTIC
NEW YORK   TORONTO   LONDON   AUCKLAND   SYDNEY
MEXICO CITY   NEW DELHI   HONG KONG   BUENOS AIRES

To Marcia Thornton Jones — a true friend in any swamp.

No part of this publication may be reproduced in whole or in part, stored in a retrieval system, or transmitted in any form or by any means, electronic, mechanical, photocopying, recording, or otherwise, without written permission of the publisher. For information regarding permission, write to Scholastic Inc., Attention: Permissions Department, 557 Broadway, New York, NY 10012.

ISBN 0-439-42441-0

Text copyright © 2002 by Debra S. Dadey.
Illustrations copyright © 2002 by Scholastic Inc.
SCHOLASTIC, LITTLE APPLE, and associated logos are trademarks and/or registered trademarks of Scholastic Inc.

24 23 22 21 20 19 18 17 16 15   13 14 15 16/0

Printed in the U.S.A.   40
First printing, November 2002

CONTENTS

SWAMP MONSTER IN THIRD GRADE

1
Jake

"You're going to get in big trouble," Nancy told her brother.

Jake splashed swamp water at his sister with his green, webbed hand. "Get out of here and leave me alone," he snapped. Jake looked past the weeds and scraggly trees of the swamp to a nearby picnic area. Four human kids about his age were eating and drinking. Jake sighed. Something about humans had always fascinated him.

"You know you're not supposed to hang out near those webless creatures. Mom says nothing good can come from it," Nancy said, looking at the kids. They had finished their lunches and were tossing a brightly colored disk around.

"I'm just looking," Jake snapped.

Nancy used her tail to scratch her nose before answering. "You're going to get in

trouble. Let's go home. I'm hungry. I bet Dad made a big pot of crawfish for lunch."

Jake looked at his sister. Her face was the same shade of green as his, but her hair hung down in messy blond strands while his stood up in dark green points.

Nancy was younger and smaller, but not afraid of anything. It wasn't that she was frightened by humans, she just didn't care much about them — unlike Jake. Whenever Jake got the chance, he swam to the edge of the swamp where he could stare at the webless creatures without being seen. Right now, they were throwing the disk high into the air for a shaggy four-legged animal to catch.

The animal leaped in the air and caught the yellow disk in its mouth. "I could do that," Jake bragged. "I know I could."

Nancy rolled her eyes. "You're nuts. Forget those creatures. They're dangerous. Remember what Cousin Dominick told us about his friend being put in the zoo. I'm going home, and if you don't want to be late for lunch, you'll come with me."

"All right," Jake said with a sigh. "I'll be there in a minute." Nancy dove into the green muddy waters of the swamp, while Jake turned back to watch the humans for a little while longer.

"Look out!" a kid yelled as the yellow disk flew right at Jake's head. Jake had just enough time to duck under the water before the disk splashed into the swamp.

"Did you see that?" a blond boy in a green shirt shouted. "There was a kid in the swamp."

A skinny boy with braces shook his head. "You're nuts, Tommy. Nobody would swim in that muddy water. It's disgusting. There's no telling what kind of weird things are in there."

"How are we going to get the Frisbee?" the girl asked.

"I'm not going in there," Tommy said.

A tall boy with dark hair shook his head and the skinny boy frowned. "I just bought that Frisbee, too. There goes half my allowance."

"You guys are such wimps," the girl said. "I'll get your silly Frisbee." The girl took a deep breath and stepped close to the swamp. She crouched at the edge of the muddy water and reached out her hand. Unfortunately, she slid on a slippery rock and splashed into the muck. When she stood up she was covered with slimy weeds.

"Oh, this is so gross!" the girl moaned.

Tommy laughed and pointed at his friend. "Hey, Emily, you look like a swamp monster."

"You guys get your own Frisbee," Emily yelled and threw a weed at Tommy. "I'm going home." The kids followed Emily out of the park. None of them noticed a green, webbed hand bubble up out of the swamp, right beside the Frisbee.

2

Carrots

Through the murky waters of the swamp, Jake watched the kids leave. He waited for at least twenty minutes to make sure they weren't coming back before creeping out of the water. Tommy's Frisbee was in Jake's webbed hand. *Ping!* The Frisbee slid to the ground. Jake's slimy hands made holding onto the Frisbee almost impossible. He dropped to the ground and scooped it up against his body.

Jake's green skin tingled. For a swamp monster to be out in the open was dangerous but exciting. If a webless creature saw him, there was no telling what might happen. Jake took a few steps toward the picnic area and tossed the Frisbee into the air. He raced toward it and tried to catch it with his hand, but his webbed fingers were just too slippery. Then Jake tried to catch it in his mouth, like he'd seen the animal do. The Frisbee bounced off his head and onto the ground.

"Ouch," Jake bellowed. "That's not as easy as it looked." Jake tried over and over again. He ran faster and faster. Finally, the fifth time Jake tossed the Frisbee, he ran and caught it in his mouth.

"I knew I could do it!" Jake said with a laugh. "I bet I could play the same game with a big clamshell." He tossed the Frisbee back in the air. It landed with a thud in a big metal trash can.

Jake picked the Frisbee out of the can and sniffed. The webless creatures had thrown away lots of strange-smelling foods and drinks. Jake tried a taste of one bottle labeled SUNTAN LOTION. He had to admit it was pretty good. The chocolate milk he spit out immediately. "Yuck!" Jake said. "How can they drink that stuff?"

Jake picked a few plastic bags out of the trash and tried the foods inside. The white stuff and meat were okay. The tuna fish was great, but it was the skinny orange things that Jake really liked. There was a big bag of them. Jake tossed some of the orange sticks up in the air and caught them in his mouth before eating them. But most of them he crammed into his mouth as fast as he could. They were crunchy and delicious.

As soon as Jake ate the last one he felt strange. His head hurt and he felt dizzy. The green color of the trees and blue of the sky blurred together and Jake fell to the ground. "What's happening to me?" Jake yelled. "Nancy, help me! Nancy!" Jake had never felt so sick. He closed his eyes and fainted.

Way out in the swamp, Nancy stuck her head out of the murky water. Jake! He was in trouble. Nancy was almost home but turned tail and raced back to where she'd last seen Jake. Nancy was the fastest swimmer in her family, but she wasn't fast enough. By the time she reached the picnic area, Jake was on the ground, surrounded by four webless creatures.

"Oh, no!" Nancy said with a gulp. "Jake is in big trouble."

Meanwhile, the girl named Emily nudged Jake with her tennis shoe.

"Is he dead?" Tommy asked.

3

Webless

Jake groaned. His whole body ached like he'd wrestled an alligator. His head still felt funny, but when he opened his eyes, he got an even bigger shock. Four webless creatures were staring at him. This was a swamp monster's worst nightmare — to be cornered. Jake looked around wildly for an escape route.

"Don't worry," Emily said. "We won't hurt you." Jake focused in on the webless creatures. They were the same four he'd seen earlier.

"It's a good thing we came back for

Ryan's house keys," Tommy said. "You might have been here for days. Not many people hang out near the swamp."

Ryan, the skinny boy with braces, stared at Jake. "What's wrong with you? You look really pale."

Jake stared down at his arms and got the

surprise of his life. Pale skin covered his body, and the webbing between his fingers was gone. He was still wearing the swim trunks he'd found on the beach two months ago, but everything else had changed. In fact, he looked like a webless creature. Jake panicked. He couldn't figure out what had happened to him.

But when Emily smiled at him, Jake felt safe. He smiled back at her. "Why don't we take you to the Eatery for a snack?" she asked. "You look like you could use a bite to eat."

Jake nodded. "Sure, I'd like that."

Emily helped Jake to his feet while Ryan searched the grass for his keys. Tommy and the tall boy helped Ryan. "Look at this," Tommy said, pointing under the picnic table. "I found the Frisbee."

"How'd that get out of the swamp?" Ryan asked.

Jake opened his mouth to tell them he'd found it but decided against it. He didn't want them to know he'd come from anywhere near the swamp.

"I'm Frank," the tall boy said. "Where do you live? I haven't seen you around before."

Jake put his hand to his head. What should he tell them? He couldn't exactly say he *lived* in the swamp. They might freak out if they knew he usually had bright green skin and scales.

"Oh my gosh," Emily said. "I think he has amnesia. I bet he hit his head and doesn't remember who he is or where he lives."

Jake grinned at Emily. That was the perfect excuse.

"Maybe we should call a doctor," Frank suggested.

Jake held up a hand. "No!" he shouted, and then more softly he said, "I just need to rest and I'll be fine." Jake didn't want anyone to examine him. They might find that some of him was still a swamp monster.

"I found them!" Ryan said, holding up a small key ring.

"Great," Frank said. "Let's get a snack at the Eatery."

Tommy nodded. "You can come over to my house afterward. I bet my mom will even let you spend the night."

"Thanks," Jake said. He couldn't believe how nice these humans were being. His cousin had told him horror stories of swamp monsters that had been put in cages after falling into the clutches of humans. Jake didn't need to be afraid of these webless creatures. Still, he'd never spent a night away from the swamp. In fact, he'd never been more than ten feet away from it. The farther the kids walked from the swamp's muddy water, the more nervous Jake became. What if he turned back into a swamp monster right in front of them?

Jake shuddered at the thought. Emily would probably faint. Tommy might faint, too, but Frank and Ryan might call the police. Jake would end up at the zoo his cousin had told him about.

By the time the five kids had gotten to the Eatery, sweat beads had formed on Jake's forehead. But a double cheeseburger, large fries, and a soda helped Jake to forget his worries. He had never tasted anything

so good. Jake gulped it all down in two minutes flat.

Emily laughed when Jake licked his fingers. "You act like you've never had a cheeseburger before," she said.

"I haven't," Jake said. Seeing the funny looks the kids gave him, he quickly added, "At least, I don't remember eating one before."

Jake's soda was empty, so he took a drink from the Tabasco bottle. It was a little spicy, but not too bad.

"Don't drink that!" Emily shrieked. "Here, take the last of my soda." Jake would rather have finished the Tabasco sauce, but he sipped Emily's soda without complaint.

While the other kids finished their food, Jake looked around the Eatery. He'd never

21

been anyplace so loud. People were everywhere, and there were loud noises coming from a black box on the wall. Kids in strange costumes rolled around with funny ball-like things attached to the bottom of their feet. "Those look like fun," Jake told Ryan. "They look even faster than fins."

Ryan looked at the in-line skaters and shook his head. "You are really weird," Ryan told Jake.

Jake gulped. Did they suspect he was from the swamp?

4

Home

"Thanks for letting me spend the night," Jake told Tommy, "even if I am a little weird." Jake sat up in a sleeping bag on Tommy's bedroom floor.

Tommy laughed. "That's why we like you," he said. "We're weird, too. You'd better get some sleep. Tomorrow we have to decide what to do about your amnesia."

"Just don't tell your parents until we figure something out," Jake said. "They seem nice, but . . ."

"Don't worry about it." Tommy tossed Jake a white fluffy thing. "They think you're here to help with my science project," Tommy said.

"Thanks," Jake said as Tommy turned out the lights and hopped into bed. In just a few minutes, Tommy started snoring very loudly. Jake laughed. Tommy sounded just like his sister, Nancy.

Nancy. Jake knew she'd be worried sick about him, along with his parents. Somehow he had to get word to them that he was okay. But how? Jake didn't even know where he was or which way he'd have to go to get back to the swamp. Tomorrow he'd get Tommy to show him the way. Then when Tommy wasn't looking, Jake could sneak into the swamp and tell Nancy what had happened.

Jake still couldn't believe it. He looked at his skin in the moonlight. It was still pale.

Would his skin always be this way? Jake had spent his whole life as a swamp monster. He wasn't so sure he wanted to be webless now.

Still, it was pretty exciting. He'd seen things that he'd never known existed. Tommy had this box in his room that held people. He used a smaller box to turn it on and off. He had another strange object that made loud music with the touch of a button. It was incredible.

Jake admitted to himself he had always been curious about webless creatures. But being curious about them and turning into one were two different things. At least he knew what the orange things were that had changed him. Tommy's father had even offered the boys some for a snack. They were carrots and Jake had quickly turned them down. He didn't want to pass out again.

Jake looked at the feathery white thing that Tommy had tossed him. It was soft, like the mud piles that swamp monsters laid their heads on when they rested. Jake put his head on the white thing. It was even softer than mud! Jake rolled over in the sleeping bag. He'd never slept outside of the swamp before. How did humans sleep in this dry, fluffy stuff? What he needed was a cup of water to make things more comfortable. Jake listened. Tommy still snored away.

Quietly, Jake walked to the bathroom. He'd watched Tommy using the sink earlier, and it was easy to turn it on with his webless fingers. The water blasted out of the sink and splashed everywhere. Jake put his hand against the faucet to try to stop it, but that only made the water squirt into his face. Finally, he figured out that he had to turn the knob in the opposite direction to get it to stop. The water came out more slowly, and he filled a paper cup with the strange-looking water. It was clear like rain, not green and murky like the swamp water.

He sloshed the strange water around inside his sleeping bag and hopped back in. Ah. That was better. Jake closed his eyes and drifted off to sleep.

In the middle of the night, Jake heard a noise. He sat up in his sleeping bag. He looked around — where was he? There were no weeds or fish. Then Jake remembered eating the carrots.

Jake heard the noise again. It wasn't

Tommy's snoring. The noise had come from outside. Jake eased out of his damp sleeping bag and peeked out the window. A green shadow stood in the yard, waving its arms at him. Jake waved back and hurried quietly through the house and out to the backyard.

"Nancy," Jake whispered. "I'm so glad you're here."

Jake's sister dripped slime all over him as they hugged. Her green face held a huge frown. "What happened to you?" she asked. "Mom and Dad are worried sick. I had to tell them you were spending the night with Cousin Dominick."

"I'm so sorry," Jake said. "I ate some orange sticks and now I've turned into a human."

"Serves you right." Nancy put her arms

across her green chest. "I told you nothing good would come from watching those webless creatures all the time. Now, just look at you. You're as pale as the inside of a clam!"

Jake pointed his webless hand at his sister. "Listen, they have some great things here. Boxes with little people inside of them, instant music, and cheeseburgers."

"So what?" Nancy said. "They still can't breathe underwater. How are you going to get back to normal?"

"I don't know what to do," Jake admitted. "What if I never turn green again?" The idea of never seeing his parents again was frightening, but he tried to be brave for his sister.

"It would serve you right," Nancy snapped, but she looked a little scared, too.

Nancy dropped her head down and Jake put his pale hand on her scaly shoulder. "We'll figure something out," he told her. "Don't worry."

5

Gills

The moonlight glowed from behind Nancy's green head. If anyone saw her, she'd be in the zoo in no time. Jake worried that Tommy or his parents might wake up, but everything was quiet. "You have to come home right now," Nancy said. "Mom and Dad will figure out that you're not really at Cousin Dominick's."

Jake showed Nancy the side of his neck. "I can't come home," he said. "I don't have gills. I wouldn't last more than five minutes in the swamp water."

"No gills!" Nancy shrieked. She rubbed

Jake's neck, but it didn't help. The gills were completely gone. Nancy looked horrified.

"Don't worry," Jake told his little sister, trying to sound a lot braver than he felt. "I'm sure this won't last forever. I bet I change back before the end of the week."

"Do you really think so?" Nancy asked.

Of course, Jake had no idea what would happen, but he didn't want his sister to get any more upset. Jake fibbed a little. "I will be back in the swamp in no time, gills and all."

This news seemed to help Nancy. "Well, I guess if you stay a little longer, you can tell me all about how humans live. I'll try to keep Mom and Dad from finding out what happened until you get back."

His sister hugged him tightly and then

pouted. "It's no fair. You always get to have all the fun." She smiled at her brother before turning to leave. "See you soon."

"Good-bye," Jake said with a gulp. He watched his sister swim toward a clump of trees, and then he heard a splash as she dived under the water. He made a mental note of which direction she went. If he ever changed back to a swamp monster, he would need to head that way fast. As his sister disappeared behind the trees, Jake wondered if he would ever see her again.

6

Squish

"I don't know if this is such a good idea," Jake told Tommy as they walked to Glenstone Elementary School. Jake had on the tennis shoes and clothes that Tommy had lent him. Jake's swimming trunks weren't right for school.

Tommy headed toward the front door. "You have to go to school," Tommy told Jake. "Or my mom will think something is wrong."

"Something *is* wrong," Jake said.

Tommy nodded. "We don't have to tell my mom that," he said. "Unless you want to."

Jake shook his head, took a deep breath, and put his hand on the door handle. "Let's get this over with."

"Okay," Tommy said. "I'll tell them you're my cousin and you're visiting for a few days. Frank did that last year with his cousin."

Fifteen minutes later, Jake sat in a third-grade classroom. Tommy sat on the other side of the room in the only other empty seat, but Emily sat nearby. The teacher, Mrs. Varga, talked about the different continents. Jake found it hard to believe there were so many people scattered all over the world. Swamp monsters didn't travel much. They had to stick together to survive. Jake tried to remember everything to tell his sister. School was pretty exciting. Jake was glad he had come.

"Now, who can name the seven continents?" Mrs. Varga asked the class.

No one answered. Jake looked around. Surely someone remembered what she had just told them. Tommy sat with his head down, doodling on a piece of paper. "Jake?" Mrs. Varga asked. "Do you know?"

Jake stood up and nodded. "Yes, ma'am. The seven continents are: Africa, Antarctica, Asia, Australia, Europe, North America, and South America."

Mrs. Varga smiled, but behind him Jake heard snickers. "Very good, Jake. You may sit down now."

Jake felt proud of himself. But when the teacher turned away a boy named Ted knocked Jake's book off his desk. Ted whispered, "The new boy is a smart aleck. Why don't you go back where you came from?"

"I can't," Jake said sadly. He felt pretty low until he glanced at Emily. She smiled at him and Jake forgot all about Ted. "Do you remember who you are yet?" Emily whispered.

Jake shook his head. "No, but I remembered the answer to that question."

Emily grinned. "I knew you were smart when I first saw you."

"That's enough whispering," the teacher interrupted, before starting a lesson about multiplication. Jake tried to pay attention, so he could tell Nancy, but something was happening to him — something weird.

His shoes felt squishy. He felt the back of his neck. Gills! Even his skin looked a little green. He was turning back into a swamp monster. Jake felt relieved until he remembered where he was.

Emily sat right next to him. Tommy was on the other side of the room. All around him third graders sat taking notes and drawing pictures in their notebooks. What would they think if the new kid suddenly turned into a green monster right beside them? Would he be able to get out of the school without being caught and taken to the Swamp Monster Zoo?

"Emily," Jake whispered. "Do you have any carrots?"

Emily looked at him. "Are you sick? You look like you're ready to pass out."

Jake nodded. "I need carrots or something terrible will happen." Jake didn't want to pass out again, but he didn't have a choice.

Emily thought Jake might be diabetic like her sister. Emily's sister sometimes needed certain foods to make her feel better. Emily grabbed her lunch box and searched. No carrots. She leaned over and whispered to a neighbor. Kids all over the classroom checked their bags and boxes. Two scraggly carrots found their way back to Emily.

"Thanks," Jake said as Emily passed the carrots over. Jake gulped the carrots down.

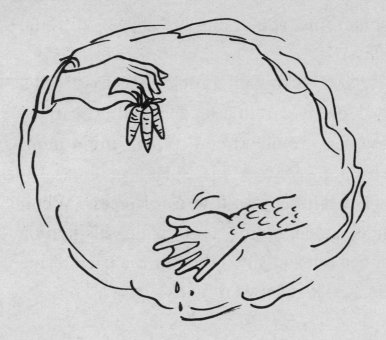

He hoped they were enough to stop the change. His eyes felt blurry and his stomach churned, but he didn't pass out. Jake felt the back of his neck. It worked. The gills were gone.

"Whew!" Jake said out loud.

"Jake?" the teacher asked. "Do you have

something you'd like to share with the class?"

"No," Jake said quickly. "Sorry." Jake was pretty sure his teacher didn't want to know her student could turn into a monster.

Everything was fine until recess. When Jake stood up to go outside, his tennis shoes felt squishy. Jake felt the back of his neck. The gills were back!

7

Bathroom

"Emily," Jake whispered in the hallway on the way to recess. "I have to have more carrots."

Emily took one look at the green color on Jake's face and knew he needed help. "Let me take you to the nurse's office," she suggested. She wished Tommy was around. Why did he have to have band practice during recess today?

Jake didn't want a nurse to find his gills. "No, please just get me more carrots. Knock on this door when you've got them." Jake ducked inside the boys' restroom just as webs sprouted between his fingers.

Unfortunately, the mean kid, Ted, was in the restroom, too. Ted threw three used paper towels toward the trash can. All three of them missed. Ted just let them stay on the floor. "How does it feel to be such a smart aleck?" Ted asked Jake.

"Actually," Jake told him, "I feel pretty sick." Jake hid his hands behind his back and hoped Ted wouldn't see his gills opening up.

"You look sick, all right," Ted said. "And I'm sick of jerks like you. You want to fight?"

Jake shook his head. "I don't want to fight you. I need to sit down." Jake tried to get inside one of the bathroom stalls, but Ted blocked his way. Every time Jake tried another stall, Ted blocked him.

"Look, Ted," Jake explained. "I'm *really* sick."

"Are you going to pass out or something?" Ted asked.

Jake didn't feel like fainting, but he could feel spikes starting to grow on his head. If Jake didn't do something fast, Ted would see a full-fledged swamp monster in the boys' bathroom.

Meanwhile, Emily had searched everywhere for more carrots. Nobody had brought any for lunch. Unfortunately, none of the cafeteria ladies were in the kitchen.

"Hello," Emily called to the empty kitchen. "I need some carrots for my sick friend."

No one answered. Emily knocked on the door of the kitchen office. "Please," she shouted. "I need some carrots. My friend

must be diabetic or something. He needs carrots right away."

Nothing. Emily didn't know what to do. She looked around and spied three huge metal refrigerators. She tugged hard on one of the doors. Inside she saw huge jars of applesauce and pickles. On the very top shelf sat a big bag of carrots. Emily was reaching for the carrots when a voice boomed from behind her. "Young lady, are you stealing from the school kitchen?"

Emily turned around to face the principal. "I wasn't stealing, Principal Pellman," Emily said. "I just needed some carrots for my sick friend."

"If your friend is sick, she needs to go to the nurse's office," Principal Pellman snapped. "If you're stealing, you need to come to my office. Now, follow me."

"But my friend isn't a girl. . . ." Emily started to explain.

"No buts," Principal Pellman said. "Follow me." Emily gulped and followed the principal out of the kitchen. They walked down the hall in silence. Emily tried to figure a way out of the mess she was in, and a way to help Jake.

As they walked by the boys' room, they heard a terrible scream. Ted ran out of the bathroom shrieking, "A monster! A monster!"

8

Monster

"What's gotten into that boy?" Principal Pellman asked. She looked at Emily. "We'll discuss the carrots later. Now, get to class." Principal Pellman raced after Ted.

After checking the hallway to make sure no one was around, Emily tapped on the boys' room door. "Jake?" she asked. "Are you okay? Jake?"

Emily heard a moan and a thump. "Jake? Is there really a monster in there?" Emily was all set to scream for help when the bathroom door creaked open slightly.

"Emily?" Jake whispered. "Do you have the carrots?"

"I'm sorry," Emily said. "I couldn't get them. I can try again."

"No," Jake whispered. "There's no time. I have to get out of here without anyone seeing me."

Emily tried to peek inside the door, but the lights were out. "What are you talking about? What's going on?"

"I need some way to get back to the swamp without anyone seeing me," Jake said.

"Are you crazy?" she asked.

"Please, Emily," Jake begged. "I really need your help."

"Did Ted hurt you?" she asked. Emily couldn't figure out why Jake would need to get out of the school without anyone seeing him, unless Ted had given him a bloody nose.

"Please, just help me," Jake whispered.

Emily sighed. "I'll get a cart and something to cover it," she said before hurrying into the library. A large audiovisual cart was parked in a corner next to huge rolls of bulletin-board paper. Emily quickly pulled off a big sheet of paper and wrapped it around the cart, leaving one side loose.

Before the librarian could spot her, Emily grabbed a roll of tape and pushed the cart down the hall. "Jake," Emily whispered into the bathroom door. "The cart is here. Jake?"

"Close your eyes," Jake said.

Emily laughed. "You've got to be kidding."

"Please, Emily. Before someone sees us."

"Oh, all right. But I still don't see what all this fuss is about." Emily closed her eyes and heard grunting as Jake squeezed himself into the bottom of the cart and pulled the paper tight around him. Emily opened her eyes and finished taping the paper shut.

"Let's go," Jake whispered. "And please hurry. I need to get to the swamp right away."

Emily nodded and tried to move the cart. She pushed with all her body weight, but the cart didn't budge. "Jake, you're too heavy. Now what are we going to do?"

Emily was trying to figure out how to move the cart when Principal Pellman and Ted walked down the hall.

9

The Great Escape

"I thought I asked you to get back to class," Principal Pellman said to Emily.

Emily gulped. "I'm taking this cart to the library," she lied. Emily crossed her fingers behind her back. She hated lying, even if it was to help Jake.

"Get on with it," Principal Pellman told Emily. "Now, Ted. Let's see this monster you're talking about." Principal Pellman knocked loudly on the door of the boys' room. When no one answered, she and Ted walked into the bathroom. In just a few seconds, they walked out again.

Principal Pellman's red face showed her anger. "Just as I suspected. This is not funny. You just earned yourself a detention this afternoon for lying."

Emily looked down at the cart but didn't say a word. "And you," Principal Pellman roared at Emily. "What are you still doing here?"

"I'm sorry, but the cart is very heavy," Emily explained.

Principal Pellman glared at Ted. "Help Emily move this cart to wherever she needs to go and then get to class. You're both in detention this afternoon." Principal Pellman stomped away to her office.

"Detention," Emily said. "I've never had detention before."

Ted laughed. "Don't worry. I get stuck in detention all the time. It's not so bad

after you get used to being cooped up in a small room with no food, no water, and no talking."

"It sounds like prison," Emily said with a shudder.

"That's why we have to have fun while we still can," Ted said. He gave the cart a strong push and jumped on the back of it. He rolled down the hall toward the back door.

"Actually," Emily said. "I do need to take this cart *outside*."

"Okay," Ted said. "I'll do anything to get out of school."

"Then you won't mind helping me push it to the swamp," Emily said.

Ted looked at Emily like she was crazy. Then he shrugged. "Hey, I already have detention. And Pellman did say to take this cart wherever you needed to go. Why not the swamp?"

Ted did great with the cart on the sidewalk, but when they got to the edge of the park where the sidewalk ran out, things got harder. Emily helped Ted push the clunky cart over the bumpy grass toward the swamp.

"Why are we doing this, anyway?" Ted asked.

"Oh," Emily said, trying to come up with a reason quickly. "It's all part of a science experiment."

Ted nodded his head like he believed her. Emily breathed a sigh of relief. Usually she was a terrible liar.

When they got to the edge of the swamp, Emily thanked Ted. "I couldn't have done it without you," she said. "But I can finish by myself."

"No way," Ted said. "I want to see this experiment for myself." Ted grabbed the paper, "Ready to pull this off?"

"No!" Emily screamed.

10

Back at the Swamp

"Leave that cart alone!" Emily shouted. "You'll ruin my experiment if you pull that paper off." She thought fast and changed the subject. "Tell me what you did to Jake in the bathroom."

Ted held his hands up in the air. "Hey, I didn't do anything to Jake. I was talking to him, and he turned into a green monster right before my eyes!"

"What in the world are you talking about?" Emily snapped.

"It's true," Ted said. "He had these pointy things on his head and webbed fingers like a . . . a . . . like a swamp monster." Ted pointed to the swamp and nodded.

Emily waved her finger at Ted. "I don't believe you and I want you to stop making up stuff about Jake. Now, just get out of here. I don't need your help anymore."

"Fine," Ted grumbled and walked away. "I knew you wouldn't believe me. See if I ever help you again."

Emily waited until he was out of sight before whispering, "Jake, are you okay?"

"Yes," came the muffled reply.

"Then come on out here," Emily demanded. "And tell me what all this craziness is about. If it weren't for you, I wouldn't have detention. Here I am at the swamp when I should be in school. I can't believe I'm doing this."

"I'm really sorry," Jake said softly.

"Then get out of there," Emily said.

"Would you mind leaving?" Jake asked.

"What?" Emily said.

"I don't want you to see me," Jake whispered.

"What are you talking about?" Emily said. "Get out here right now." She jerked the paper away from the cart.

Jake was hunched over, but he looked very different. He had green skin with webbed hands and feet. His eyes were yellow and spikes grew where his hair used to be.

"Stop this fooling around!" Emily yelled. "Take off that costume and let's get back to school where we belong."

"I don't feel very well," Jake said softly.

"I think I've been out of the swamp too long."

Emily grabbed one of Jake's spikes and pulled. It was stuck fast. She tugged at his skin. "Oh my gosh," Emily squealed. "It's real. You really are a monster!"

11

The Rescue

Jake fell out of the side of the cart and landed on the ground with a thump. "Jake?" Emily said. He didn't move. Emily didn't know what to do. She looked at Jake's green skin. She didn't want to touch him again, but she couldn't just leave him there on the ground.

With one finger Emily poked Jake's arm. "Jake, wake up."

Jake lifted his head weakly before passing out again. "I could just leave," Emily said to herself. "No one would know that I was here, except for maybe Ted. And nobody would believe Ted." Emily shook her head. She couldn't do it. Jake was her friend. She had to help him.

Emily took a deep breath and pulled on Jake's arm. He was really heavy. Emily grabbed both arms and yanked as hard as she could. Jake barely moved. "What if I can't get him back in the water?" she said. She pulled and pulled, but she only got him a foot closer to the swamp.

Emily slapped Jake's face gently. "Come on, Jake," Emily cried. "You have to wake up." Jake slumped over face-down on the ground.

Emily pulled again and again, but Jake moved only a few inches. Finally, she fell to the ground exhausted. Emily hadn't cried in a long time, but she was desperate. For all she knew, Jake might be very sick. She put her face in her hands and started sobbing.

"Stop crying and give me a hand," a voice said.

"Jake?" Emily said, looking up. It wasn't Jake, though. It was a green girl with stringy blond hair.

"Ahhhhh!" Emily screamed and fell backward. She couldn't believe she was seeing another swamp monster. It was like a nightmare!

"Shhhh. I'm Nancy, Jake's sister. Please help me get him back into the water." The two girls grabbed Jake's hands and tugged together. They pulled him across the muddy ground and into the slimy water.

Nancy grinned at Emily. "Thanks. I can take it from here." Nancy grabbed Jake under his arms and dragged him deeper into the swamp. When they were neck-high, Nancy pulled Jake under the water.

"Wait," Emily said. "Is he okay? Will I ever see him again?"

But the only answer Emily got was the bubbles coming up out of the swamp. Finally, even the bubbles disappeared.

12

Friends

"I can't believe it," Emily told Tommy as they walked toward the swamp later that day.

"Maybe you were dreaming," Tommy told Emily. "It's a good thing Frank and Ryan had basketball practice. They'd think you were crazy."

Emily kicked at a rock on the sidewalk. "I didn't make up detention. I definitely had that. No, the whole thing was real. Jake is a swamp monster."

Tommy rolled his eyes and wondered if Emily was coming down with the flu. He'd heard that people sometimes started to see crazy things when their fever got too high. Just today, Ted had said he'd seen something weird in the boys' bathroom.

Emily pointed to a spot where the grass was smashed down flat. "This is where he fell to the ground. You should have seen him. He was green all over."

"Maybe Jake is the Jolly Green Giant's nephew," Tommy teased.

"You think I'm making it up, don't you?" Emily said.

Tommy shrugged. "Well, you have to admit the whole thing sounds pretty nutty."

Emily stomped her foot. "I know what I saw. Jake was right here and he was sick. Another swamp monster helped me put him in the water. I just hope I did the right thing. What if he drowned?"

Suddenly, a green webbed hand touched Emily's arm. "You did the right thing," Jake said.

Emily jumped.

"Jake!" Tommy yelled. Tommy couldn't believe his eyes. Jake really looked like a swamp monster. He *was* a swamp monster.

Tommy stared, but Emily grabbed Jake and hugged him.

"Thank goodness you're okay," Emily said. "I was so worried."

Jake grinned, showing his orange teeth. "You saved my life."

"How? What? When?" Tommy asked, feeling slightly dazed. He wondered if he had the flu, too.

Jake handed Tommy his wet clothes and shoes before telling them the whole story of how the carrots had changed him. "Once I was back in the water I was fine. My parents were pretty upset about the whole thing. I'm grounded for life."

Emily laughed. "My parents would be upset if I left home to live in the swamp."

Tommy gulped and looked at the murky

water. "You mean there's a whole family of swamp monsters living in there?"

"Of course," Jake said solemnly. "There are lots of families. But don't tell anyone. If you do, we won't be safe."

"We won't tell anyone," Emily said, giving Tommy a serious look.

"Think fast," Jake told Tommy, before throwing a Frisbee. "I found another one in the swamp."

Tommy caught the Frisbee and tossed it back. Jake raced to the Frisbee and caught it in his teeth.

"Awesome!" Emily said with a laugh.

Tommy laughed, too. "Can you teach me to do that?"

Jake shrugged. "Sure. It was cool being a webless creature, but the swamp is my home. It's where I belong."

Jake turned and walked back toward the water. "Wait," Emily said. "Will we ever see you again?"

Jake grinned. "As long as there are carrots, you never know what will happen."

About the Author

Debbie Dadey is the author and co-author of more than one hundred books, including the Adventures of the Bailey School Kids series. The idea for *Swamp Monster in Third Grade* came from a Bailey School book, *Swamp Monsters Don't Chase Wild Turkeys*.

Debbie lives in Colorado with her husband, three children, and two dogs. It's usually very dry in Colorado, so she hasn't seen any swamp monsters lately. But she's keeping an eye out for them.

Ready for some spooky fun? Then check out this brand-new series from best-selling authors, Marcia Thornton Jones and Debbie Dadey!

Ghostville Elementary

The basement of Sleepy Hollow's elementary school is haunted. At least that's what everyone says. But no one has ever gone downstairs to prove it. Until now . . .

This year, Cassidy and Jeff's classroom is in the basement. But the kids aren't scared. There's no such thing as ghosts, right?

Tell that to the ghosts.

The basement belongs to another class — a *ghost* class. They don't want to share. And they will haunt Cassidy and her friends until they get their room back!

#1
Ghost Class

Cassidy stumbled over to the wall and flipped on the light switch. She spun around to see a boy about her age, sitting in her desk. He had dark hair that stuck up on top. He wore denim overalls and a striped shirt with a collar. She stared at his tattered shoes until his laughter made her look into his brown eyes.

"How did you do that?" Cassidy asked the boy, but he wouldn't stop laughing. "That wasn't funny at all," she told him.

She stepped toward the desk. "You'd better quit laughing," she warned. She reached over to grab him, but her hand closed around nothing except air — very cold air.

Cassidy's mouth dropped open as she hugged her own dusty arms. She had never felt such a chill. For the first time, Cassidy noticed that the boy wasn't normal. He shimmered around the edges. He was so pale that Cassidy could see right through him. He reminded her of a glowing green-frosted bubble. The boy stood up from the desk and in that instant, he disappeared.

"Where did you go?" Cassidy asked. "Come back here."

The room was still except for a whisper. "I'm warning you. Leave my desk alone."

At first, Cassidy was scared. Had she really seen a ghost? Then Cassidy got mad.

Dust covered every surface of the classroom. Mr. Morton would think she did it. "Come back here and clean up this mess!" Cassidy stomped her foot, sending a little dust cloud into the air above her sneakers. She may as well have been talking to the wind, because the boy didn't reappear.

"This is just great," Cassidy snapped. "Some kids get pen pals — I get a ghost bully."

Suddenly, a noise made Cassidy freeze. Maybe the ghost was back! She whirled around. Jeff and Nina stood at the door to the playground.

"Did you guys see that?" Cassidy asked.

"See what?" Jeff and Nina said together.

"The ghost boy," Cassidy told them.

Jeff laughed. "Yeah, right. I think I just saw a ghost boy skateboarding around the playground."

Nina put her hand on Jeff's shoulder. "I think she's serious. Cassidy really saw something."

"I'm serious, too." Jeff said with a grin. "Serious about the trouble Cassidy's going to be in when Mr. Morton sees this mess. Maybe the Ghostville ghost can help you blast this mess away," he teased.

Cassidy glared at Jeff as she stomped to the back of the room to grab a mop. "I'm not joking," she said. "I just saw a ghost right here in this very classroom."

Jeff tossed a dust mop to Cassidy. "Next you'll think that mop is a dancing skeleton."

"It's not fair," Cassidy mumbled as she swished the mop across the floor. "Not fair. Not fair. Some ghost made the mess and I have to clean it up. Not fair. Not fair. Not fair."

Cassidy stomped on the mat by the back door extra hard. She was so mad she didn't notice that something weird was happening — the little rug underneath her feet was bunching up all on its own. It wiggled, it squirmed, it bubbled, it scrunched. Suddenly, Cassidy teetered. Then she fell down right on the seat of her pants.

From somewhere in the empty basement came the sound of laughter. . . .

Creepy, weird, wacky, and funny things happen to the Bailey School Kids!™ Collect and read them all!

The Adventures of THE BAILEY SCHOOL KIDS

Available wherever you buy books, or use this order form

Scholastic Inc., P.O. Box 7502, Jefferson City, MO 65102

Please send me the books I have checked above. I am enclosing $_____ (please add $2.00 to cover shipping and handling). Send check or money order — no cash or C.O.D.s please.

Name _____

Address _____

City_____ State/Zip_____

Please allow four to six weeks for delivery. Offer good in the U.S. only. Sorry, mail orders are not available to residents of Canada. Prices subject to change.

THE SECRETS OF DROON

A Magical Series by Tony Abbott

Under the stairs, a magical world awaits you!

- ❏ BDK 0-590-10839-5   #1: The Hidden Stairs and the Magic Carpet
- ❏ BDK 0-590-10841-7   #2: Journey to the Volcano Palace
- ❏ BDK 0-590-10840-9   #3: The Mysterious Island
- ❏ BDK 0-590-10842-5   #4: City in the Clouds
- ❏ BDK 0-590-10843-3   #5: The Great Ice Battle
- ❏ BDK 0-590-10844-1   #6: The Sleeping Giant of Goll
- ❏ BDK 0-439-18297-2   #7: Into the Land of the Lost
- ❏ BDK 0-439-18298-0   #8: The Golden Wasp
- ❏ BDK 0-439-20772-X   #9: The Tower of the Elf King
- ❏ BDK 0-439-20784-3   #10: Quest for the Queen
- ❏ BDK 0-439-20785-1   #11: The Hawk Bandits of Tarkoom
- ❏ BDK 0-439-20786-X   #12: Under the Serpent Sea
- ❏ BDK 0-439-30606-X   #13: The Mask of Maliban
- ❏ BDK 0-439-30607-8   #14: Voyage of the *Jaffa Wind*
- ❏ BDK 0-439-30608-6   #15: The Moon Scroll

$3.99 each!

Available Wherever You Buy Books or Use This Order Form

www.scholastic.com

SD402

SCHOLASTIC